Bantam Books in the Choose Your Own Adventure® Series
Ask your bookseller for the books you have missed

#1 THE CAVE OF TIME
#2 JOURNEY UNDER THE SEA
#3 BY BALLOON TO THE SAHARA
#4 SPACE AND BEYOND
#5 THE MYSTERY OF CHIMNEY ROCK
#6 YOUR CODE NAME IS JONAH
#7 THE THIRD PLANET FROM ALTAIR
#8 DEADWOOD CITY
#9 WHO KILLED HARLOWE THROMBEY?
#10 THE LOST JEWELS OF NABOOTI
#11 MYSTERY OF THE MAYA
#12 INSIDE UFO 54-40
#13 THE ABOMINABLE SNOWMAN
#14 THE FORBIDDEN CASTLE
#15 HOUSE OF DANGER
#16 SURVIVAL AT SEA
#17 THE RACE FOREVER
#18 UNDERGROUND KINGDOM
#19 SECRET OF THE PYRAMIDS
#20 ESCAPE
#21 HYPERSPACE
#22 SPACE PATROL
#23 THE LOST TRIBE
#24 LOST ON THE AMAZON
#25 PRISONER OF THE ANT PEOPLE
#26 THE PHANTOM SUBMARINE
#27 THE HORROR OF HIGH RIDGE
#28 MOUNTAIN SURVIVAL
#29 TROUBLE ON PLANET EARTH
#30 THE CURSE OF BATTERSLEA HALL
#31 VAMPIRE EXPRESS
#32 TREASURE DIVER
#33 THE DRAGONS' DEN
#34 THE MYSTERY OF THE HIGHLAND CREST
#35 JOURNEY TO STONEHENGE
#36 THE SECRET TREASURE OF TIBET
#37 WAR WITH THE EVIL POWER MASTER
#38 SABOTAGE
#39 SUPERCOMPUTER
#40 THE THRONE OF ZEUS
#41 SEARCH FOR THE MOUNTAIN GORILLAS
#42 THE MYSTERY OF ECHO LODGE
#43 GRAND CANYON ODYSSEY
#44 THE MYSTERY OF URA SENKE
#45 YOU ARE A SHARK
#46 THE DEADLY SHADOW
#47 OUTLAWS OF SHERWOOD FOREST
#48 SPY FOR GEORGE WASHINGTON
#49 DANGER AT ANCHOR MINE
#50 RETURN TO THE CAVE OF TIME
#51 THE MAGIC OF THE UNICORN
#52 GHOST HUNTER
#53 THE CASE OF THE SILK KING
#54 FOREST OF FEAR
#55 THE TRUMPET OF TERROR
#56 THE ENCHANTED KINGDOM
#57 THE ANTIMATTER FORMULA
#58 STATUE OF LIBERTY ADVENTURE
#59 TERROR ISLAND
#60 VANISHED!
#61 BEYOND ESCAPE!
#62 SUGARCANE ISLAND
#63 MYSTERY OF THE SECRET ROOM
#64 VOLCANO!
#65 THE MARDI GRAS MYSTERY
#66 SECRET OF THE NINJA
#67 SEASIDE MYSTERY
#68 SECRET OF THE SUN GOD
#69 ROCK AND ROLL MYSTERY
#70 INVADERS OF THE PLANET EARTH
#71 SPACE VAMPIRE
#72 THE BRILLIANT DR. WOGAN
#73 BEYOND THE GREAT WALL

#1 JOURNEY TO THE YEAR 3000 (A Choose Your Own Adventure Super Adventure®)

BEYOND THE GREAT WALL

BY JAY LEIBOLD

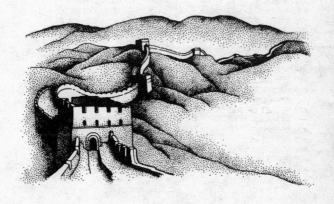

ILLUSTRATED BY YEE CHEA LIN

An R. A. Montgomery Book

BANTAM BOOKS
TORONTO · NEW YORK · LONDON · SYDNEY · AUCKLAND

RL 4, IL age 10 and up

BEYOND THE GREAT WALL

A Bantam Book / August 1987

ISBN 0-553-26725-6

Published simultaneously in the United States and Canada

PRINTED IN THE UNITED STATES OF AMERICA

O   0 9 8 7 6 5 4 3

BEYOND THE GREAT WALL

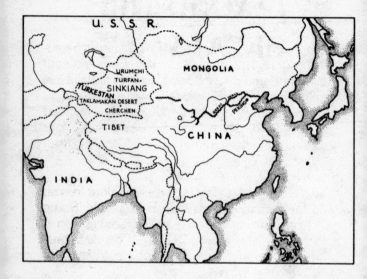

WARNING!!!

Do not read this book straight through from beginning to end. These pages contain many different adventures you can have as you try to find the lost archaeologist Dr. Pinckney and win the reward offered by Baron von Frothingham. As you read along you will be able to make choices. Your choices will determine whether or not you succeed.

You will face many difficult choices in your travels, and meet many different kinds of people. Some will help you and some will not. You are responsible for your fate because you make the decisions. After you make a choice, follow the instructions to find out what happens next.

Be careful! You are going to a forbidding and dangerous part of the world.

Good luck!

HISTORICAL NOTE

Many of the adventures in this book echo actual experiences of European archaeologists in Sinkiang in the first part of the twentieth century.

Sven Hedin (whom you meet in one adventure) was the first to venture extensively into the Takla Makan Desert. His purpose was to explore and survey the area, but on the way he discovered several ancient sites. This began a race among the European countries, as well as Russia, Japan, and the United States, to uncover the art and manuscripts of the lost civilizations of the Silk Route.

Perhaps the most famous of these archaeologists was Sir Aurel Stein. After investigating ruins in the Lop Desert and finding the long-lost western extension of the Great Wall, he was led to the Caves of the Thousand Buddhas near Tun Huang. The caves were tended by an abbot named Wang. Stein befriended Wang, in part through shared admiration for the pilgrim Hsüan-tsang. He managed to convince Wang to let him excavate some of the caves and carry off several donkey-loads of manuscripts and other artifacts to England.

Other adventures in the book with an historical basis include the manuscript forgeries of Akhzur, the Rat King of Khotan, the Tungan guerrillas, and the Russian exile Boroshin. The story of Fan and Meng is drawn from a legend of the Great Wall.

Two years ago, in 1899, Baron von Frothingham, an avid collector of Buddhist art and antiquities, sent his agent Dr. Pinckney to China to locate a cave filled with treasures. Pinckney has not been heard from since. The baron has put up a sizable reward for finding Dr. Pinckney, and you aim to win it.

Sunk deeply in a leather armchair in the baron's library, you listen intently as the baron recounts the events leading up to Pinckney's disappearance. Also listening are eight other adventurers and fortune-seekers, most of them quite unsavory in appearance. You all will be competing for the reward.

The baron, a jolly, rotund man with a big curling mustache, obviously enjoys the luxuries of life. "According to our information," he says, "the Cave of a Thousand Buddhas contains great quantities of antiquities of exquisite quality. Paintings, frescoes, sculptures, vases, manuscripts over fifteen centuries old. I know it's hard for a cutthroat lot such as yourselves to appreciate these things, but to me, they're like gold."

Turn to page 2.

"Naturally, my foremost concern is Dr. Pinckney's safety and well-being. However," the baron goes on, his eyes burning, "I want to find that cave. Therefore, the reward will be given for finding either Pinckney or the cave."

Turn to page 10.

The baron pauses, a faraway look in his eye. "Now," he goes on, "Pinckney was to meet our informant in Turfan. There they would negotiate. Then Pinckney would be taken to the Cave of a Thousand Buddhas, which, as far as we could tell, is somewhere near the western end of the Great Wall."

The baron holds up a photograph of a large man with wide eyes. "This is a picture of Dr. Pinckney. I'll pass it around so all of you can see it. Are there any questions?"

"What was Dr. Pinckney's route?" you ask.

"Well, ahem," the baron replies, "I know he was planning to go through India, over the high passes of the Karakoram Mountains, and cross the Takla Makan Desert. He wanted to investigate some other sites along the way. Unfortunately, I don't know if he took the southern branch of the Silk Route, or the northern. I don't bother with such details."

After the briefing is over, the other adventurers rush off to London to begin travel preparations. But you wonder if you should go to Cambridge first and visit your friend Professor Montgomery. The professor is an archaeologist who may be able to give you some helpful information about Sinkiang and the Takla Makan.

If you go to Cambridge to see Montgomery, turn to page 20.

If you leave as soon as possible for China, turn to page 110.

But when you wake up, Ford and Hickey are gone. You find out that they decided to leave most of their gear behind and try to make it to Cherchen with what they could carry themselves. You're glad to be rid of them, but now you're stranded with no money at all. You wonder if you'll ever get out of the Takla Makan.

A few days later a westbound caravan provides the way. You're hired on as a camel-tender. You stay with the caravan all the way through to Persia, where you find Montgomery and tell him he was right after all.

The End

"It sounds interesting," you say.

Montgomery sighs. "I can see you're determined to go. Well, I have to admit it's a fascinating area. The study of Chinese culture is not my specialty, but I've always been intrigued by it. With your desert experience, and your knowledge of languages, you probably have as good a chance as anyone to succeed. By the way, how are you going to pay for this expedition?"

"I have some money saved," you answer.

"But I'll bet you could use a little help," Montgomery says. "Since so few scientists get into—or out of—Sinkiang, perhaps . . ."

"Go on," you urge.

"You see, I hate to imagine any more artifacts falling into the baron's hands than already have. If I gave you some additional funding, would you keep an eye out for interesting sites along the way?"

You smile. "I was hoping you'd propose something like that."

Turn to page 14.

"Excuse me," you say, rushing out of the dining room. But there's no hurry. The Chinese man is pretending to read a newspaper in the lobby. You stride out onto the street, knowing he will follow you.

You duck into a mosque and hide behind a pillar. When the man peers in, you grab him by the collar, push him against the wall, and demand to know why he's been trailing you.

"Let me go," he gasps, "and I'll tell you."

You're surprised by his English. You let go of his collar, and he says, "I've been following you because you're the only one I can trust."

"What?"

"My name is Jonathan Chan," he says, extending a hand. "I'm part of a group in China called the Red Star. We're working to overthrow the rulers of the dynasty and set up a democratic government."

"What does that have to do with me?" you ask, still suspicious.

"We have some important, ah, information concerning Dr. Pinckney," Chan replies. "We can help you find him."

"Why would you want to help me?"

Go on to the next page.

"There are two reasons. One is that we want part of the reward, but we can't risk exposing our organization. The other is that we want to get these European fortune-seekers out of Sinkiang before they ransack and pilfer any more ancient ruins.

"You were the only one of the riffraff from the baron's home who looked trustworthy," Chan continues. "When I saw you go into Professor Montgomery's house, that was another point in your favor. Still, I had to make sure. When you started talking to the two in the hotel—"

"They're no friends of mine," you interrupt.

"That's reassuring. Now, this is my proposition. I have contacts in Ansi who I believe will be able to lead us to Dr. Pinckney. If we succeed, all I ask is that you leave Pinckney alone, and split the reward with us. Are you interested?"

If you say, "Yes," turn to page 36.

If you say, "No," turn to page 18.

The baron brings forward a map of Asia. "This is where you'll be looking," he says, stabbing the center of the map. "In the Chinese province of Sinkiang, also known as Kashgaria, Tartary, Chinese Turkestan, and heaven knows what else. It's the meeting point of three major empires—the Chinese, the Russian, and the British in India.

"For centuries it was part of the old Silk Road, the trade route that connected China to India, Persia, and, indirectly, to the Roman Empire. Marco Polo traveled it. It's mainly a basin of bleak deserts surrounded by the highest mountain ranges in the world. Yet a string of oases grew up along the road to support the silk trade.

"This road was also a principal route of Buddhism and Buddhist art from India to the Far East. The pilgrim Hsüan-tsang, for instance, brought manuscripts back to China from India in the seventh century. Monasteries and temples, supported by travelers, sprang up along the road.

"But then, in the thirteenth century, these pockets of civilization began to disappear. Partly this was because the rivers were drying up. Mainly, however, it was because China was conquered by Genghis Khan and later, during the Ming dynasty, cut itself off from the rest of the world. Slowly the desert swallowed up the kingdoms, towns, and monasteries along the old Silk Route. The important thing—for us—is that the dry climate has preserved the treasures of this civilization better than any museum could have. They wait only to be discovered."

Turn to page 4.

You thank Jasik, and ride off with five of his clansmen toward the Great Wall. You follow a trail up through the hills to the base of the wall.

No border guards are in sight, but still you must figure out how to get over the massive stone structure. One of the Mongols, seeing your worried look, says, "Don't worry. My people have a long history of getting over the Great Wall."

The six of you set to work building a long ladder. When it is ready, the Mongols hold it while you climb shakily to the top. At the parapet of the wall, you wave good-bye and cry, "Thanks!"

They wave. Before they ride off, one calls to you, "We have heard there is another foreigner living on the other side. Maybe he can help you!"

You pull the ladder up to the parapet, and maneuver it over to the other side. You climb down, and hide the ladder in the trees.

Not far down the valley you come across a little hut. "Hello!" an old man cries in a Russian accent.

You find out that his name is Boroshin. He invites you in for a meal. As you eat, you learn that he has exiled himself here after being caught planning a revolution in Russia. He lives a lonely, simple life in the hills. He listens eagerly as you sit by the fireside and tell him news of the world. Then you explain to him why you are there.

"Well," he says, "I may be able to help you. A foreigner recently arrived in this area. He may or may not be Dr. Pinckney, but it is worth checking. He is staying at the monastery a little way down the hill from here."

Turn to page 88.

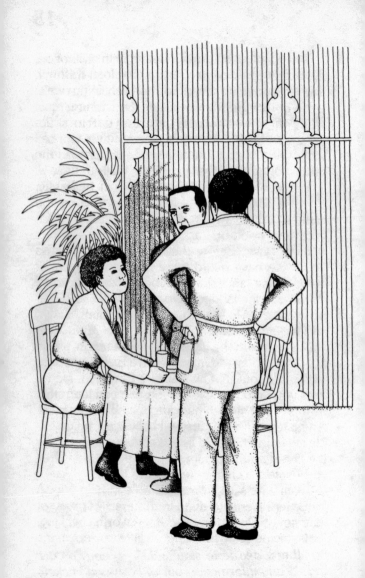

You decide that for your last night in civilization, you'll treat yourself to a stay in the Hotel Kashmir. As you sit down to dinner in the hotel dining room, you catch sight once again of the Chinese man who seems to be following you. You start to get up to confront him, but at that moment two men hail you. You recognize them as men you saw in the baron's library. They pull chairs up to your table as if you're an old friend. You sit down hesitantly, trying at the same time to keep an eye on the Chinese man in a mirror.

"I'm Lucas Ford," one of the fortune-seekers says. He has a thick mustache, narrow eyes, and is dressed in safari clothes. "This is my partner, Harrison Hickey. We've joined forces to find Pinckney. Why don't you come along with us?"

"No thanks," you say. "I work alone."

"What about your visit to Professor Montgomery?" Ford insists. "Don't tell me he didn't help you. Are you going to give him a cut of the reward?"

"How'd you know about—hey, is that man over there—" You turn to point to the Chinese man, but he's gone!

If you jump up and chase after the Chinese man, turn to page 8.

If you decide to stay and see if you can get any information out of Ford and Hickey, turn to page 64.

"I might have known," Montgomery says, smiling. "Now we just have to work out your route."

"I thought the quickest way would be to sail to China and go overland from there," you say.

"Normally, yes, if it weren't for the Boxer Rebellion. But this happens to be a very bad time to be a foreigner in China. Missionaries and diplomats especially have a hard time of it, but anyone from the West could be a target. I can't say I blame the Chinese. Our governments have been bullying them for the past sixty years with unfair trade agreements. A group that Westerners call the Boxers is simply striking back. Things shouldn't be as bad in Sinkiang, though."

"Which way would you go, then?"

"The fastest way may be to go through Tsarist Russia," Montgomery says. "You can take a train to Omsk, then get to the Chinese border by whatever means you can find.

"But," he goes on, "that's not the best way. You may have passport trouble in Russia. Although it's the slowest, the best way is through India. Go by ship to Bombay, up through Srinagar, and over the mountains to the Takla Makan. Besides, if you go that way, you may be able to trace Pinckney's steps.

Go on to the next page.

"No matter which way you go," Montgomery concludes, "you must know how to protect yourself, especially while crossing the Takla Makan. Don't take weapons. In my experience, unless they're traveling in a large expedition, the travelers who get themselves killed are the ones who think they can fight. Instead of weapons take along plenty of medicines—not for yourself, but for the local people. It's the best way to make friends."

If you say, "I'll take the India route,"
turn to page 111.

If you want to go by way of Russia,
turn to page 79.

"I'll test the bridge out first, and if it holds, everyone else can come over," you declare.

Chan says nothing, so you go on down to the snow bridge. But before you can start across it, Norzen pushes you aside, saying, "Let me go. I can listen to the snow."

You watch as Norzen inches delicately over the bridge. Everyone lets out a breath of relief when he reaches the other side. "The snow is pretty solid, but it's slippery. Be careful," he warns.

You come next, leading the pony laden with the balloon. Gingerly you edge across. But the pony is not stable on the snow. In the middle of the bridge, one of its legs slips out from under it. You turn to see it sliding off the snow bridge. You grab the pony's mane, but the animal is too heavy for you to hold back. You're pulled over the edge with the pony and the balloon, and swept away in the icy current below.

The End

You go to bed. You'd rather get your sleep than risk the desert at night.

The caravan plods on across the Takla Makan. The sun is unbearably hot and dry. Sometimes you feel bored. But at other times you enjoy exchanging stories with the caravaners, or listening to the clanging of the camel bells and the songs of the camel-tenders, or playing games with the horsemen.

Finally you reach Turfan, where the caravan disbands. You say good-bye to the prince, and begin asking around the city for information. But you learn nothing of the cave or of Pinckney. Your last hope is a merchant you're told to see, named Akhzur.

Akhzur greets you in the local custom, taking both your hands, stepping back and bowing slightly, then stroking his beard in a graceful motion. You do the same, though you have no beard to stroke.

Akhzur's eyes light up when he hears that you're interested in ruins. He takes you into the back of his shop, where ancient manuscripts full of strange characters are piled in every corner.

"I found them in buried cities in the Lop Desert," he tells you. "Very old, very valuable. But I can sell them to you for a good price."

Turn to page 37.

Chan looks disappointed. "I wish you felt otherwise. But I shall honor your decision. Good night."

You return to the hotel. Early the next day you buy the rest of your supplies and hire a guide. Then you set off across the Karakoram to catch the caravan in Kashgar. The mountain crossing is difficult but uneventful, and you arrive in Kashgar just as the caravan is preparing to depart. It is led by the prince of Bezeklik, who says he is honored to have you accompany him.

The caravan leaves in the morning. It's an amazing sight. An old woman in a cone-shaped, fur-brimmed hat is near the front, followed by a string

of two hundred and fifty camels kicking up dust in the red light of dawn. They're flanked by forty horsemen with ancient rifles strung across their backs or with broadswords at their sides.

The caravan follows the northern arm of the Silk Route, but as far as you can tell, the only markers on the route are the piles of bones of animals and people who didn't make it. Every day you start before dawn, rest during the worst heat of the afternoon, and sometimes continue in the evening. At the end of the day, there is chaos as the camels are unloaded, boxes are piled everywhere, and tents are pitched haphazardly.

Turn to page 24.

"Ah, it's my young adventurer friend," Professor Montgomery exclaims when he opens his door. He's a large, bearded fellow with crow's-feet around his eyes. "Come in. I've been wondering what kind of trouble you've been getting into lately."

You settle yourself with a cup of tea in the garden behind Montgomery's house. "As a matter of fact," you say, "do you know the baron von Frothingham?"

"Heard of him," Montgomery replies warily, lighting up his pipe. "I've met his associate, Pinckney. Frothingham sent him on some wild-goose chase in China a couple of years ago."

"Exactly," you say. You explain about Pinckney's disappearance and the baron's reward. "So that's why I came. I thought you'd have some advice for me about traveling in Sinkiang."

The professor puffs on his pipe, his brow furrowed. "My advice is that you shouldn't go. In the first place, chances are that Pinckney was killed, and you won't find him. In the second place, chances are that that's what will happen to you. I'm mounting an expedition to Persia. Why don't you join me? I'll pay a fair wage."

"Thanks," you say. "But the baron's reward is too good to pass up. What's so dangerous about Sinkiang, anyway?"

Go on to the next page.

"To begin with, the Takla Makan Desert. Oh, I know you're an experienced desert trekker. You showed me that in Egypt on my last expedition. But the Takla Makan is the most unforgiving desert on earth. Its name in Turki means 'go in there and you won't come out.' The temperature gets above one hundred and twenty degrees in the summer, and down to forty below in the winter. Water is almost impossible to find, even when you know where to look. And the *burans*—huge sandstorms—come without warning and can swallow you up. Whole caravans have disappeared."

"Still," you insist, "it must be possible to get through."

"It's possible," Montgomery concedes. "But you also have to deal with bandits. If not bandits, then spies—the Chinese, Russians, and British like to keep an eye on each other there. And if not spies, then rebel fighters. Fifteen years ago, there was a Moslem uprising in which thousands of people died. Ninety percent of the people in Sinkiang Province are non-Chinese. They're Uighurs, Kazakhs, Kirghiz, Mongols, and other Turkish races, and they resent Chinese rule. Not that the government has much control. It's a desolate, lawless place, somewhat like the American West."

Turn to page 6.

You follow the old road on this side of the Great Wall, and, just as you expect, it leads you to a monastery.

You take a deep breath, knock on the door, and describe the coat to the monk who answers. The monk looks at you as if you're crazy. But he allows you into the courtyard, where he tells you to wait for the abbot.

As you sit waiting, another monk walks across the courtyard. Something about him looks familiar.

"Dr. Pinckney!" you blurt out.

The monk looks up involuntarily. He hesitates, then decides to talk to you. "My name—my former name," he corrects himself, "was not Pinckney, it was Smith. What brings you to our monastery?"

Turn to page 34.

One night you're invited to tea with the prince in his tent. You ask about Pinckney and the Cave of a Thousand Buddhas, but he knows nothing. However, he tells you tales of lost cities in the desert, of buried rooms with painted men and demons.

"Where are these places?" you ask.

"There are ruins just a little way south of our camp," the prince says. "But don't go out there. The demons come to life at night."

You're curious about the buried cities. In spite of the prince's warning, you start thinking about going into the desert to investigate.

If you decide to look for the ruins, turn to page 32.

If you decide you'd better not risk it at night, turn to page 17.

The next morning, you pack up and begin the long trip to the Great Wall. You travel through deserts, staying away from cities and roads where you might be questioned by Chinese officials.

A couple of months later you finally reach the road to Tatung. When you come into the hills near the Great Wall, you decide to stop and ask an innkeeper about the weeping stone.

The innkeeper knows immediately what you're talking about. "Yes, the weeping stone is part of the wall. But you do not want to go there," he warns. "The place is haunted."

"How would I get there?" you ask.

"The old Tatung road leads right to the spot," he says. "The road has been abandoned because the place is cursed." He warns you several times against following it, but you ignore his warnings.

Although the road is faint and overgrown with bushes, it leads you right to the Great Wall. There you find water trickling from a stone in the wall, even though you haven't seen rain for weeks.

You push at the stone. It swings open, allowing you to enter a dusty chamber inside the wall. As you step inside, the stone swings closed behind you. You light a candle, and nearly jump out of your shoes from fright. A row of skeletons leans against the wall, grinning at you.

Suddenly it becomes hard to breathe in the chamber. You push desperately at the stone, trying to get out. But it won't budge. You sit down, exhausted, and feel yourself losing consciousness.

Turn to page 82.

"I don't want to buy any manuscripts right now," you say to Akhzur. "Where are these buried cities?"

He waves vaguely. "In the Lop Desert, on the edge of Lop Nor."

You replenish your supplies and in a couple of days head into the Lop. The first thing you see is a mass of Mongol horsemen, dressed for battle, coming over a ridge. Startled, you pull your pony back. But as you watch, the teeming mass changes, and you realize you're seeing a mirage.

You trek through the desert to the edge of Lop Nor, the salt bog and lake that swallows the rivers and civilizations of the desert. Following the edge between the desert and the bog for several days, you finally find the tip of a wooden structure sticking out of the sand.

You set up camp and begin to dig. Suddenly the sand starts rushing into the structure beneath you. You try to climb away but you're drawn down in the sandslide. You land in a heap.

You find that you've slid into an underground labyrinth. Using matches to light your way, you explore the maze of corridors. The walls are covered with paintings of deities and demons preserved by desert dryness.

You keep exploring, fascinated by the world unfolding before your eyes. You're so absorbed that you don't notice the sliver of light ahead of you. You gasp when you stumble into a tiny dome-shaped room, illuminated by a shaft of light coming from somewhere above. Sitting in the room is a man deep in meditation.

Turn to page 40.

Meanwhile, two Russian men, acting very secretive, take the berth across from yours. They leave you alone, though, and you decide not to worry about them. You sit back and watch the landscape as the train chugs through Siberia.

In Omsk you switch to a boat, which takes you down the Irtysh River. You notice that the two Russian men are also on the boat, but they don't seem at all interested in you.

Until Semipalatinsk, that is, when you get off the boat and find yourself in the same carriage with them, bound for the Chinese border. The smaller of the two men, whom you heard the driver call Mr. Mirmsk, looks you over, then asks, "Where are you going?"

"I'm going to see the Great Wall of China," you respond. "I'm writing about it for a magazine in London."

"A worthwhile subject, wouldn't you say, Pogolosky?" he says to his companion.

"Which part of the wall are you visiting?" Pogolosky asks you.

"I'm starting at the western end and working my way east."

"Ah, very nice," Mirmsk says, and that seems to be the end of it.

You spend the night at an inn. The next morning, as you prepare to hire a horse to ride to Urumchi, you notice something awry with your luggage. You don't think anything about it until Mirmsk corners you and demands, "So where is Pinckney?"

Turn to page 53.

As you steer south toward Tun Huang, you see a strange pattern in the desert below. It looks like a line of some kind drawn straight across the landscape. You drop down to take a closer look.

"It's like a long dirt mound, right through the middle of the desert," you say.

"But every so often there's a square tower or something rising out of the mound," Chan notes.

"It's almost as if it were once a wall," you say. "It couldn't have been an extension of the Great Wall, could it?"

"Yes!" Chan cries. "It's quite possible! The annals speak of a long-lost western section of the wall. Perhaps we've found the remnants of it. That would be a major discovery!"

"Maybe someone in Tun Huang will know about it," you say.

You soon land in Tun Huang, where it doesn't take long to recover from the altitude sickness. Chan wants to move on to Ansi, but you say, "Let's just ask around a little about the Great Wall."

Chan agrees, reluctantly, to split up and spend the morning making inquiries. You find an old man in the bazaar who remembers stories about the Great Wall being near the town. He also tells you that there is a cave somewhere in the area called the Cave of a Thousand Buddhas!

You can't wait to tell Chan. But before you get the chance, you hear bad news: Ford and Hickey, the two adventurers you met in Srinagar, have just arrived in Tun Huang. What if they also know about the cave?

Turn to page 51.

"So you *were* working for the baron, the Russians, the British, *and* the Red Star group?" you ask.

"You can see why things got complicated for me," Pinckney says. "The devil of it was, I could see that *all* sides were right—and wrong. I soon realized I couldn't live with so many contradictions. I managed to escape the various parties who were searching for me. I came to the monastery in an attempt to resolve, or at least come to terms with, the contradictions. Here, I've found the life I want to lead, and I would be very grateful if you did nothing to disturb it."

"I promise we won't," you say. "But it would be nice if we could collect the baron's reward."

Pinckney thinks for a moment. "I believe that can be arranged," he says. "I'll be back shortly."

Turn to page 49.

You take some candles and strike out toward the desert ruins the prince described.

The desert is an eerie place at night. You feel as if you're on another planet. Nothing is familiar, except the quarter moon low in the sky.

After a couple of hours of walking, you spot a dark structure half-buried in a sand dune against the horizon. You can see how the dune, moving as a slow, windblown wave, first covered the building, and now is moving past it. You dig the sand away from a half-exposed door until you can pull the door partway open. You go inside.

It's pitch-dark. You light a candle. The room is littered with fallen beams, pieces of crockery, and utensils from a thousand or more years ago. As you look them over, you notice another door in the back of the room. You tug on it, but it's stuck. After a lot of pushing and pulling, it suddenly flies open.

You enter the room, holding the candle in front of you. Immediately you jump back with a gasp. The ancient skeleton of a horse, barely touched by your hand, crumbles to dust. You find yourself looking into the blank eye sockets of three mummified Buddhist monks against the wall behind it. From the other three walls you're watched by wild-eyed demons.

You back out of the room and pull the door closed. But then you hear something. You stop and listen. A rattling sound is coming from somewhere in the building.

Turn to page 46.

You decide that the best thing to do is to tell all you know and hope that Pinckney, or whoever he is, can help. The abbot arrives, and you tell your story, beginning with the meeting at the baron's house and ending with the dream at the chamber of the weeping stone. "And now I'm here to find the coat," you say.

The monk looks at the abbot. The abbot thinks for a while, then says, "The coat is here. We will give it to you. You should take it to the chamber and leave it there. Please return and tell us what happens."

An apprentice brings you the coat, and you set off for the wall. Soon you are back at the weeping stone.

You push open the entrance, and lay the coat in the middle of the chamber. You wait. Nothing happens. You wait a while longer, worried that you haven't done something right.

Finally you decide you must leave. You push the stone open again. As you do, you sense something behind you. You look back. Two doves spread their wings and fly out of the chamber, disappearing high into the sky.

Turn to page 67.

Partway down the pass you come to a place where there is supposed to be a bridge across a torrent of glacial water. Norzen shrugs his shoulders and says, "Bridge washed away. We have to go back up the pass and take the other route."

You're out of breath from the high altitude and hard climbing. "You mean we have to climb back up the pass and go down another way? What a waste of time," you object.

Norzen nods, saying, "Yes. And the other route is two days longer."

"There must be a better way," you insist. Looking ahead, you see a thin bridge of snow spanning the river. You point to it and ask Norzen, "Will it hold us?"

He shrugs. "Maybe. Only one way to find out for sure."

"Wait a minute," Chan objects. "Some of these ponies are packed very heavily. That snow looks too weak. It's not worth it. Let's go back up the pass."

You look at the bridge, then back up at the steep face you've just come down.

If you say, "You're right, we'll have to go back up the pass," turn to page 38.

If you say, "Let's try to cross the bridge," turn to page 16.

"Excellent," Chan replies. "Now, shall we return to the hotel and discuss this like civilized people?"

Back at the hotel you're glad to see that Ford and Hickey have gone. You sit down to dinner, and Chan tells you about his group, Red Star, which is trying to change the Chinese government.

In the morning you and Chan hire a guide to take you over the Karakoram Range. Then you shop for the rest of the gear and supplies you'll need.

Turn to page 42.

The manuscripts look intriguing. Maybe you should buy as many as you can to take back with you. You could give some to Montgomery, and maybe even sell some at a profit to the baron.

On the other hand, you think, you could go into the Lop Desert and investigate those places yourself. The only problem is that you may not be able to find the ancient sites, and you're weary of desert travel.

If you decide to buy some manuscripts, turn to page 77.

If you decide to go into the Lop Desert, turn to page 27.

38

You climb up the pass and go down the longer route. You trek for two more weeks until, finally, you enter the Gez defile, a long valley leading all the way down to the Takla Makan.

As you descend into the foothills you begin to feel the heat of the desert. It's hard to believe it can be so hot, after the cold and snow of just a few days ago. A yellow haze that had hidden the desert now clears away. Far below, you can see crest after crest of sand dunes stretching to the horizon like the waves of a petrified ocean. You can also see a few irregular ribbons of silvery water. These are the rivers that come out of the mountains only to disappear, sucked up by the desert. On the edge of the brown dunes are a few patches of oasis green.

In Kashgar, you pay Norzen and his assistants. He wishes you luck with what he calls "your crazy balloon plan," and leaves with the ponies.

The next day you and Chan begin to assemble the balloon outside of town. A throng of curious onlookers gathers, asking all kinds of questions. They've never seen anything like this.

At last the balloon is inflated and ready to go. You pack your supplies, including plenty of water, into the gondola. Then you and Chan climb in. You check the flaps and untie the anchor ropes. The balloon rises into the air.

Turn to page 104.

Your eyes open. You get up and look all around for Fan, thinking he was sitting right next to you. But you see only the grinning skeletons leaning on the wall, and you quickly remember where you are.

You're now desperate to escape. Once again you push at the stone. Nothing happens. Then you begin to push at the stones on the far side of the chamber. Suddenly one swings open. You're on the other side of the wall!

You can breathe again. You sit down, and your dream comes rushing back to you. You feel as if you know exactly where the monastery with Fan's coat is. But maybe the whole thing is just a trick of the deathly air in the chamber.

If you head for where you think the monastery is, turn to page 22.

If you think you shouldn't waste time, and decide to look for Pinckney instead, turn to page 102.

The man looks up when you enter. There's an expression, or lack of expression, on his face that you've never seen before.

"Who are you?" he wants to know.

You tell him, then ask, "How did you get down here?"

"Down where?"

"Here, under the ground," you say.

"Ah." He thinks about this for a moment. "Apparently it has been a long time. When I began my meditation, this room was a hidden part of a monastery that was most certainly above ground. I suppose the desert has come and reclaimed it."

The man proceeds to ask you questions about Chinese history. You're able to answer most of them because of the reading you did before you left London.

"So it has been more than a thousand years," he comments. At your disbelieving look he explains, "When you enter a state of ecstasy, extinguishing every concrete thought, the body becomes irrelevant. It may not die for thousands of years."

With awe you realize you're talking to an *arhat*, a Buddhist saint, who went into a trance, and has sat, unnoticing, for hundreds of years as the desert sands covered the world around him.

Turn to page 99.

You grit your teeth and stand up. Sand gets in your eyes, ears, and nose, and it's almost impossible to breathe. But you manage to adjust the gas and make the balloon rise. Higher and higher it goes, in the grip of the storm. A blast of wind nearly flips it over, but you hold on.

Suddenly you're clear. You and Chan open your eyes. Below, the black storm swirls. But above and all around is clear—but very thin—air.

"We must be up awfully high," Chan says. "I feel like I can't get enough air in my lungs."

"Me, too," you say. "But we can't go back down. We'll just have to wait it out."

It seems like hours before the storm lets up.

By the time you're able to start down, you and Chan both show symptoms of high-altitude sickness. You let the balloon drop as fast as you dare.

"I can't quite tell where we are," Chan says, looking at a map and the compass. "But I'm pretty sure that if we head due east, we'll reach Ansi."

You glance at the map. "Ansi's still pretty far away," you say. "Look, there's another town south of here called Tun Huang."

"Oh, no. I don't think we should go to Tun Huang. I know my friends in Ansi can help us."

For some reason Chan is set against going to Tun Huang. But you wonder if it's wise to try to make it all the way to Ansi.

If you insist on steering toward Tun Huang, turn to page 30.

If you agree to try for Ansi, turn to page 50.

42

In one of the bazaars you buy some used equipment from an Englishman in a tattered officer's uniform who has just returned from an expedition. He says his name is Douglas Haley. He has a long skinny head, big sideburns, and he's covered with bruises and bandages. "Where are you going?" he asks.

"We're crossing the Takla Makan Desert," you say.

"Hmm, then perhaps you'd be interested in buying a used balloon. It's in very good shape, only has a few thousand feet on it. I'll accept any reasonable offer."

"I doubt it would help us across the Takla Makan," Chan says.

"On the contrary!" Douglas Haley replies. "There's no better way. You'll get there ten times faster than on a pony. And you won't have to fool around with stubborn camels or slog over endless sand dunes. The only thing I'd advise against is trying to fly it over the mountains. I attempted to make the first balloon crossing of the Himalaya. As you can see, I was not entirely successful."

"How would we get it over the Karakoram?" you ask.

"Simple," Haley answers. "Pack it over on a pony. I'll even give you free flying lessons before you leave."

Turn to page 78.

A group of curious monks gather around your balloon. Chan steps out of the gondola first and asks to see the abbot.

When the abbot appears, Chan gives him the name of one of his friends. The abbot nods and ushers you to a small room inside the monastery. Soon a large man with gentle, wide eyes enters and sits down.

"Dr. Pinckney?" you ask.

"Yes," the man says with a sigh. "That is my former name. I suppose I should have expected this."

"Don't worry," Chan says. "We have no intention of exposing you."

You tell Pinckney your story, starting with the baron's reward, then meeting Chan, buying the balloon, and following the Great Wall to the monastery.

Pinckney nods to himself as you speak, and when you're finished, says, "I guess I have nothing to lose by telling you my story. As you know, I originally came to China to dig up artifacts for the baron. I set out for the Cave of a Thousand Buddhas, but never made it there.

Go on to the next page.

"In my former business, one sometimes must play several different roles, especially when working in the province of Sinkiang. Archaeology was my main purpose. But I also worked as an agent for the Russian government, sending them information about the local political situation and the activities of the British, Chinese, and Japanese. But I wasn't *really* working for the Russians—I was actually a double agent for the British."

Chan looks shocked. "But I thought you were working for us!"

"I was," Pinckney says with a trace of weariness. "Your associates convinced me of the validity of your cause. They helped me to decide not to divulge to Europe the location or contents of the Cave of a Thousand Buddhas. But then things started falling apart. The Russians and the British were after me, and so was your group."

Turn to page 31.

You run outside. To your dismay, the moon has gone down, and the desert is almost as dark as the room had been. But all you want to do is put distance between you and whatever else is in the ruins. You begin to run.

When you're finally out of breath and far enough away to relax a little, you start to wonder if you're going in the right direction. You realize that in your panic you didn't pay attention to which way you were running.

You peer ahead in the darkness. You can see very little, and there are certainly no landmarks. The desert is more empty and unfamiliar than ever.

All you can do is strike out in the direction that feels right. You walk and walk, but nothing seems to change. Desperately you listen for sounds from the caravan. You think you hear them. But when you move toward the sounds, you find nothing. You realize you're hallucinating. Other strange sounds—howling wolves, moaning voices, laughter—mingle with the desert wind.

Daylight comes, and still you have no idea where you are. You decide you must choose a direction and stick with it. You do not realize until much later that you're going deeper and deeper into the Takla Makan, and you won't ever come out.

The End

"Let me explain," Chan says. "The cave, as you know, contains manuscripts, paintings, and other artifacts that are necessary for studying the past. The present Chinese government is completely unaware of the need to preserve and protect these things. Foreign devils—pardon me, but that's the term our scholars use—like the baron and his agents, or these Ford and Hickey characters, come in and plunder the sites. They deprive us of our own past."

"But wait a minute," you object. "Why aren't Chinese archaeologists out discovering these things? A lot of them would never have come to light without Europeans."

"That's true," Chan admits. "Some things have been saved that might otherwise have been lost or destroyed by robbers. Nevertheless, they belong to China, not to the West. Once the revolution occurs, we will give these sites the proper attention. Our scholars will look at the cave soon enough. I ask you to leave it alone."

You tell Chan you need a little while to decide what to do. He goes to the teahouse to wait, and you sit down to think. You're a little reluctant to leave the cave unexplored when you're so close to it. But maybe you should be satisfied with the discovery of the wall for Montgomery and—you hope—finding Pinckney for the baron.

If you agree with Chan's point and want to continue to search for Pinckney, turn to page 54.

If you decide you cannot pass up the chance to look for the cave, turn to page 66.

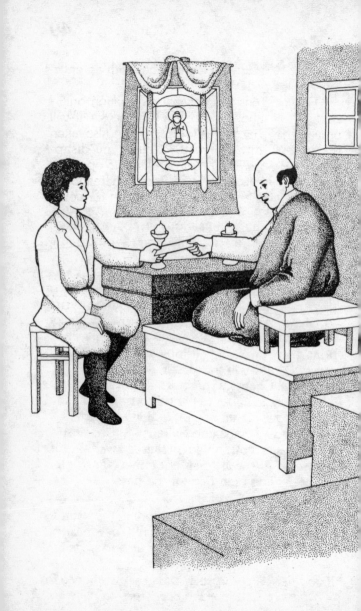

Pinckney returns in ten minutes with an envelope sealed with wax.

"The letter inside contains information only I could know about the baron," he says. "It will prove to him that you've found me. I've also taken the opportunity to try to explain my disappearance to him. If you will agree not to open the envelope, and not to give away my whereabouts, then I believe this will earn the reward for you."

You agree happily to Pinckney's request. After staying the night at the monastery, you and Chan fly the balloon to Peking. Chan proposes that you leave him the balloon, and in return he'll pay your fare back to England. You're happy to accept.

You stand on the dock, waiting to board your ship. "I'm sorry to see you go," Chan says. "We made a good team. But of course you must collect the reward."

"And send half of it to you," you remind him.

The End

50

Weak and dizzy, you barely make it to Ansi, where you crash-land. Someone finds you a doctor, and Chan sends for his friends. You spend a few days recovering at their house.

One morning, after you both feel better, Chan has a long meeting with his friends. You go out to repair the balloon and stock up on supplies. After the meeting, Chan finds you working on the balloon.

"My colleagues are very suspicious of foreigners," he says with a smile. "It was not easy to convince them to trust you, but in the end I did."

"What about Pinckney?" you ask.

"Pinckney is in a remote monastery beyond the Great Wall. It was only two days ago that my friends discovered the exact location. All that remains is for us to fly there in our balloon."

You take off the next morning, flying east to Kanchou, where you spot the western part of the Great Wall. Navigating by the wall, you follow its twists and turns through the hills of Kansu and across the yellow Ordos Desert.

In the western provinces, the wall is, for the most part, no more than a dirt mound eroded by the wind. But on the other side of the Ordos, it becomes a solid stone structure, stretching for hundreds of miles over river and mountain.

Chan tells you when to turn south for the monastery. By now you're a skilled balloonist, and you make a perfect landing in the courtyard of the monastery.

Turn to page 44.

You meet Ford and Hickey in a teahouse. "Have you had any luck finding the cave or Pinckney?" you ask.

"The cave's nowhere near here," Ford says confidently. "We got a tip that it's a hundred miles north. You'll understand if I don't divulge the exact location."

"Of course," you say, starting to leave. "Well, good luck."

"Wait a minute," Ford calls. "I've got a proposition." You return to the table but don't sit down. "We've got problems. We lost our horses in the desert, and we're getting low on money. We hear you have a balloon. We'll share the reward with you, if you fly us to the cave in the balloon."

"No thanks," you say, and quickly leave.

You find Chan back at the balloon. He's worried when you tell him that Ford and Hickey are in Tun Huang, then excited to hear that his theory about the wall may be true. But he looks stricken when you tell him about the cave.

"What's the matter?" you ask.

"I have to admit I've known the location of the cave all along," Chan says.

"You *knew*?" you exclaim.

Turn to page 47.

52

In the dead of night, you slide silently out of your blankets and crawl into the shadows. When the guard is looking the other way, you take off into the night. You grope your way down a ravine in the moonlight, knowing that, as long as you go downhill, you'll be heading in the right direction.

The sun rises, and the day heats up quickly. Soon you're sweating. But you dare not stop. You come out of the foothills, into the desert.

All day you stumble through the heat. Desperately thirsty, you stop and dig for water. You find nothing but damp sand, and realize you're wasting energy. You keep going.

Night comes as a relief, cooling off the sand. But before long you're shivering in the wind. You lie down and spend a cold, restless night.

The next day you keep trudging. Mirages of cool waterfalls and green oases dance in the heat. Your tongue and lips are cracked and dry. Again cold night comes, and you collapse in sleep.

The next day, you're thrilled to discover footprints. Then you realize they're your own, and your despair deepens. You've walked in a circle.

Your force yourself to keep moving. At last you see a cleft in the dunes. It's a riverbed!

You run down its banks, only to discover that it's dry. You drop to the sand. Your eyes close, but you know that if you don't open them now, you never will. Somehow you find the strength to get up and follow the riverbed. You walk for hours. And then you hear water.

Turn to page 73.

You're surprised, but you manage to say coolly, "Who?"

"Dr. Pinckney, the man you are tracking down for your friend Baron von Frothingham."

Now you realize what happened to your bags—Mirmsk and his friend Pogolosky searched them. "I have no idea where Pinckney is," you say icily. "Perhaps you can tell me, since you seem to know so much." Mirmsk makes no reply to this, so you go on, "Obviously you know why I'm looking for Pinckney. Now suppose you tell me why you are."

"It has been a pleasure talking to you," Mirmsk says in a formal tone. "I am afraid we must be on our way. I hope we will meet again."

After they've left, you wonder who Mirmsk and Pogolosky are. They make you nervous. You think maybe you should take a less-traveled route through the Tien Shan Mountains. If, like you, the Russians plan to search Sinkiang for Pinckney, you'd prefer to stay as far away from them as you can.

On the other hand, they may know more about Pinckney than you do. You could tail them very cautiously and see what you can find out.

If you decide to follow Mirmsk and Pogolosky, turn to page 95.

If you decide to take a less-traveled route, turn to page 93.

"I guess you're right," you say when you join Chan in the teahouse. "Finding the forgotten part of the Great Wall is a big enough discovery. Let's find Pinckney next."

Chan bows. "I appreciate your understanding."

You spend the night at an inn, and wake with the dawn to get going before Ford and Hickey. But as you approach the balloon, you see in the dim light that they've beaten you to it. They're in the balloon, loosening the anchor cables!

You run at them full speed. Ford sees you and yells at Hickey, "Quick! Get that thing untied!" The balloon starts to rise just as you reach it. With a headlong leap you plunge into the balloon gondola. You're upside down in the basket, and the balloon is rising.

"Get the legs! The legs!" Ford cries. They grab you by your legs, and lift you up, preparing to throw you out of the balloon. But you have one big advantage over them—you know how the balloon works. As they lift you, you manage to turn off the gas, causing the balloon to plunge to the ground. It hits hard, sending all three of you partway out of the gondola. By the time Ford and Hickey recover their senses, Chan is there with a group of townspeople to haul them off to jail.

"Are you all right?" Chan asks.

"I think so," you say. "I just got some cuts and bruises. Let's see if we can fix the balloon."

The balloon is easily repaired, and soon you and Chan are on your way to find Pinckney.

The End

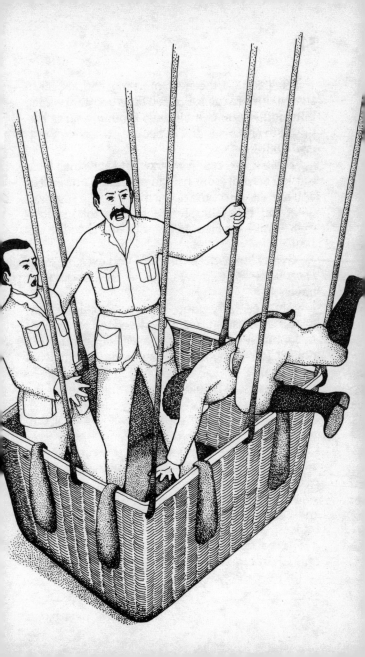

56

You pack up the next morning and set off in search of more ruins. For two days you see nothing but sand. Then, coming over a dune, you're surprised to find a handful of people dressed in Western clothes.

"Hello!" you call. A man writing at a small table outside his tent looks up. He seems as surprised as you are. As you come down the dune, he stands to greet you. He's fairly short and wears thick spectacles. "I'm Sven Hedin," he says in a Swedish accent.

"Sven Hedin, the explorer?" you exclaim. "I've always wanted to meet you. I've read about your travels."

"Ah, well. Very good," he says, a little disconcerted. "I must say, we considered ourselves bold to venture into the Lop with a well-supplied expedition. To meet you traveling alone is somewhat humbling."

"Of course it wouldn't be possible without the surveys you've already done," you respond.

"I suppose that's true," Hedin allows. "Will you join us for dinner?"

The dinner is a welcome break from your diet of *tsamba* (a doughy paste made from barley meal). You and Hedin discuss your travels for hours. Finally you ask if he knows anything of Pinckney or the Cave of a Thousand Buddhas.

Go on to the next page.

"Nothing on Pinckney," he replies, "though we did hear of his disappearance. But I may know the location of the cave you want. There are said to be some rock temples not too far from here, near Tun Huang. Tun Huang is situated in a small green valley. From what I have heard, if you follow the valley ten or twelve miles southwest, you will find these caves."

You can barely contain your excitement as you ask, "What is the best way to get to Tun Huang from here?"

"Just cut across the Lop Nor," Hedin says. "Desert travel seems to pose no problem for you."

"That's foolish," objects Islam Bai, Hedin's assistant. "Lop Nor is full of quicksand and bogs— and ghouls, some say. You should go south, around Lop Nor, then follow the Silk Route east to Tun Huang."

Hedin shrugs. "The shortest way is through Lop Nor. If I were you, that's how I would go."

If you decide to cut across Lop Nor, turn to page 62.

If you decide to go the long way, turn to page 80.

In the morning, you hike to the little monastery on the other side of the lake. You explain who you are, and Pinckney agrees to talk to you. "But," he insists, "we must talk in the woods, in secret."

You take a walk in the woods with Pinckney, and he tells you his story. "Yes, it's true, I was an agent for the British. And the Russians. And, I have to confess, also for a Chinese group working to overthrow the dynasty. It was difficult for me because all of them seemed to have valid points. As you can imagine, things got sticky."

"Is that what brought you here?" you ask.

"Basically, yes," he replies. "I also needed a place to hide until I figured out what to do. But now I know. Some friends have arranged for me to enter a remote monastery on the other side of the Great Wall. The only problem is Macarthey. I don't think he really understands my predicament. It's not his fault, he's just following instructions. But I have to figure out a way to slip past him. Will you help me?"

Pinckney's request takes you by surprise. As you hesitate, he adds, "I can provide you with proof for the baron that you found me."

If you want to help Pinckney, turn to page 81.

If you think you'd better tell Macarthey everything, turn to page 98.

You wait until the middle of the night, then creep silently out to the caves. You collect all the manuscripts you can carry, but you take nothing else. You hope Wang will realize your intentions are scholarly, not destructive.

You load the manuscripts onto one of the donkeys, and set off at a fast pace for Tun Huang. You arrive at dawn. A couple of hours later you go to the bazaar to try to find a way to return to Srinagar. There you run into Ford and Hickey!

"Well, well," Ford snickers, "it's our friend the deserter."

"If it weren't for your incompetence . . ." you begin, but then decide it's not worth going into. You're curious, though, as to how they got away from the Tungans.

"As a matter of fact," Hickey tells you, "*you* helped us. We used your money to pay off the Tungans, and they let us go. How did you get here?"

"Some shepherds picked me up in the desert," you reply.

"Well, you're a long way from the Cave of a Thousand Buddhas," Ford says. "We got a tip that it's a hundred miles north of here."

Go on to the next page.

You're glad to hear that someone has fed them false information about the cave. "I guess that's my bad luck," you say.

"We might be willing to forgive you," Ford goes on, "and let you join up with us again."

"Forgive me!" you snort. Yet, for a moment, you're tempted to take them up on their offer because you have no money. Then you remember what did happen to your money and say, "Never in a million years. Good-bye."

"Hey, what's on the donkey?" Hickey calls as you walk away.

"Nothing," you answer without turning your head.

Turn to page 87.

In the morning you thank Hedin for his help, and head out toward Lop Nor. You come to the edge of the wide salt lake within a few hours, and skirt south through the marshes. You must watch out for venomous snakes and insects as you bush-whack through the reeds.

You make it through the marsh, only to find that you must now cross a river to get back to the open dunes. The river looks shallow, though, and not difficult to cross.

You start in on your pony, with the camel carrying your supplies tethered behind. Almost immediately the pony's forelegs plunge deep into the riverbed. He sinks in farther and farther. The water is up to his belly before you realize that you're in quicksand!

It's all you can do to scramble off the saddle before you, too, are sucked in. You watch help-lessly from the bank as your pony and the camel are swallowed up. Now you are stranded in the Lop Nor with no supplies, and you will be lucky to get out alive.

The End

You turn back to Ford and Hickey, who are staring at you. "Never mind about that man," you say. "He's not important."

You talk with Ford and Hickey through dinner. You learn only that they're not well-prepared to cross the desert, but they are confident that they'll find Pinckney.

After dinner you go to your room to look over your maps. A knock comes at the door. You open it. Ford and Hickey are standing there. "What can I do for you?" you ask.

"Aren't you going to invite us in?" Ford says.

Turn to page 69.

One day Jasik wakes up with terrible stomach pains. Montgomery's advice about medicine comes back to you. "There's something in my baggage that can help you," you say. You give him some pills, praying they'll work.

They do. From that moment on you're doctor to the whole clan. People come to you with everything from minor aches to incurable diseases. You become a part of the clan. Besides your medical duties, you help out with the flocks. You pick up more of the language, and tell the people about life in your country.

You learn more about them. The clan lives a typical nomadic life, going from pasture to pasture with their sheep, cattle, horses, and camels. Sometimes, if things get bad, they raid a caravan or a traveler like yourself.

One day Jasik tells you, "Winter is coming. It is time for us to journey east to Urga, to the ancestral grazing lands. You must get ready."

You nod to Jasik. But later you begin wondering if you should go with them. You're sure you could escape at any time, but you're not sure it's a good idea. You'd have little in the way of money or supplies, though Montgomery's friend Macarthey in Urumchi might help you. If you travel with the Mongols, you may hear something about Pinckney, and at least you'll have food and shelter.

If you decide to go east with the Mongols, turn to page 94.

If you decide to escape before they leave, turn to page 96.

"I'm sorry," you say to Chan when you find him in the teahouse. "I must look for the cave."

"I'm sorry, too," he says coldly. "I guess we have nothing more to say to each other." He walks out of the teahouse. You follow and watch silently as he packs up his belongings and leaves.

The next morning you sneak out of town to look for the cave, making sure Ford and Hickey don't see you. You search everywhere for a path leading to it. But you can't find one. So you go back into town to ask if anyone knows how to get to the cave. No one seems to have any idea of its exact location, even the old man who first told you about it.

Then all of a sudden it dawns on you that this is Chan's doing. He has spread the word to keep the route to the cave secret from you. Realizing you won't get any help from the people in town, you decide to go up in the balloon and search from the air.

You go back to where you left the balloon—but it's not there! People nearby tell you that your other friends, Ford and Hickey, left in it earlier in the day.

You're stuck. You have little money left, and your transportation has been stolen. You have no choice but to join up with a westbound caravan that comes through town. You're not able to collect the baron's reward. You must be consoled with Montgomery's excitement several months later when you tell him about discovering the western extension of the Great Wall.

The End

You return to the monastery and tell the abbot exactly what you saw. He looks satisfied. "The doves," he explains, "were the souls of Fan and Meng. When the coat was returned, their souls were reunited. You have done well."

He sends for the monk who heard your story. He's eager to hear what happened. "So your story has a happy ending," he says, pleased.

"What about your story?" you ask.

The monk smiles. "I might as well admit that I am indeed the Pinckney you're looking for. I won't bother telling you how I ended up here. It's a mundane story compared with yours. But I will tell you that this is where I intend to stay and start a new life of contemplation.

"In the meantime," he goes on, "I imagine you're worried about your reward. I have a proposal: if you agree to share the reward with the monastery, and agree not to tell anyone where I am, I'll give you a letter that will prove to the baron that you've found me. Not only that, the monastery will pay for your return to London, via Peking."

You're happy to agree to his terms, and the next day you set off with an escort for Peking.

The End

Reluctantly you let them in. Hickey immediately spots your maps, and begins eyeballing them. Ford stands in front of the door. "What is it?" you say curtly.

"We just wanted to give you a chance to reconsider your decision. I think we'd make a pretty good team. We can pool our resources and split the reward three ways."

"I'm sorry, the answer is still no," you say and sit at the desk in the room.

"Please," Hickey says from behind you. "We beg of you." There's something menacing in his voice. You turn to look at him. He's coming toward you with a large hunting knife!

"Well, since you put it that way . . ."

Ford smiles. "We thought you'd see our point. Shall we shake on it?"

You offer each of them a limp hand. "Now we're partners," Ford says. "But we'll need a little insurance to make sure we stay that way."

Ford and Hickey proceed to turn your room upside down, taking your maps, papers, and money.

"Be ready to leave first thing in the morning," Ford says as he's leaving. "And don't worry, one of us will be watching your door all night to make sure nothing happens to you."

Turn to page 90.

The trip back to Khotan is long and hard. None of you has much money, and you must ration the supplies. But you make it with help from people in the oases.

On the way, you and the Turkis become fast friends. They feel sorry for you when you tell them you'll have to give up looking for Pinckney and the Cave of a Thousand Buddhas. They tell you there are many ruins outside of Khotan, and offer to take you to them.

Remembering Montgomery's request, you accept the Turkis' offer. You spend a month unearthing sites near Khotan. You enjoy the work, especially when you make an important find. At a site in the little hills surrounding the city, you discover a portrait of the sacred Rat King of Khotan.

Turn to page 89.

You manage to fall asleep, and the next morning Wang takes you on a full tour of the caves.

Now, in the daylight, with time to linger, you're even more amazed than you were the night before. Wang is especially eager for you to see paintings of the legendary adventures of Tripitaka. One shows him forcing a dragon to return a horse it had swallowed. Another shows a giant turtle coming to help carry Tripitaka's manuscripts across a raging torrent.

All during the tour, Wang goes on about how every bit of his time and money goes into painstakingly restoring the caves. "It seems the work will never end," he says with a sigh.

You know you will have to approach him carefully about removing anything. You start out by saying, "I have many friends back home who would be as excited as I am to see the manuscripts Tripitaka brought back."

Wang is cautious. "It would be bad for too many people to know about this place, especially if they do not understand Buddhism. These caves are sacred, and I must protect them."

You understand Wang's fears. Suddenly you realize that you cannot tell the baron about the caves. In his enthusiasm—or greed—for art objects, he would certainly destroy them.

Turn to page 116.

At the first rifle report, your pony bolts. You have to concentrate on staying on the pony, so you don't see what happens. But you hear it—a furious volley of firearms, mixed with yells and the whinnying of horses.

When your pony finally tires, you stop and look around. You see nothing but desert. Then, from behind some rocks, you hear, "Psst!"

You approach cautiously. Hidden in the rocks are the three Turki helpers and two of the camels. "Are you all right?" you ask.

They nod and ask about you. "I'm fine," you say. "Where are Ford and Hickey—and the bandits?"

The Turkis shrug. "Who cares?" one says. "We're going to hide here tonight, and start back to Khotan in the morning."

You agree that that's a good plan. The next day, on the way, you take a side trip to look for Ford and Hickey. You see no sign of them. Not wanting to linger too long in case the bandits return, you head back to your party. On the way, you spot something gleaming in the dust. It's Ford's rifle. You leave it where it lies.

Turn to page 70.

You rush to the sound of water and plunge your face into a pool. When you've drunk all you can, you collapse in exhaustion.

You wake up to find that you're rocking to and fro on the back of a camel. Walking behind you are three shepherds with their flocks.

"We found you at the water hole," one of the shepherds says. "We're taking you to a monastery on our way to Tun Huang. They'll take care of you there."

Still a little delirious from heat exhaustion, you arrive two days later at a small monastery built into a mountain. You thank the shepherds for saving you, and wish you had something to give them to show your gratitude.

The monks take you into a cool room and tell you you must get some rest. Slowly you return to health under their nursing.

One morning you wake up to find a small, shy man with leathery skin and lively eyes sitting by your side. "My name is Wang," he says. "I hope I am not intruding. I heard that you were dreaming of the Cave of a Thousand Buddhas."

You must have mentioned the cave in your delirium. You nod and say, "It's the reason I've traveled here."

Wang suddenly seems guarded. "Where have you traveled from?" he asks.

"From England," you answer. Wang's face shows you that this means nothing to him, so you say, "I came across mountains and the sea, and followed the Silk Route across the desert."

Turn to page 108.

"Hey, you—" Ford says angrily as you knock away his rifle.

"What's going on?" Hickey demands.

"Don't shoot!" you command. "It'll only get us killed."

By that time a squad of men on horseback have surrounded you. Hickey lays down his rifle. The rest of your small caravan is rounded up, and you're all marched to a camp in the foothills above the desert. Your captors look like a ragtag, but fierce, guerrilla group.

You soon find out that they're Tungans, Chinese Moslems in rebellion against the Peking government. They accuse you of being English spies. You protest that you're just archaeologists. "Why, then, were you about to shoot at us?" the leader asks.

You're held in captivity, unsure of what the Tungans are going to do with you. You think it might be unwise to stay around to find out. Ford and Hickey have already gotten you in enough trouble. You want to get away from them and the Tungans both.

You're pretty sure you could slip away at night. But how good would your chances of survival be alone, on foot, in the desert?

If you try to escape, turn to page 52.

If you decide to stay and hope you're released soon, turn to page 76.

It's too risky to go out in the desert alone and on foot, you decide. You'll just have to hope for the best.

One morning Ford and Hickey shake you out of sleep and tell you that the Tungans are going to let all of you go. "Don't ask questions," Ford commands. "Just get ready."

Soon you're riding out of the camp. The Tungans wave a friendly good-bye. Later in the day, you ask Ford what changed their minds.

"You're lucky you're with experienced travelers like us," he answers. "Hickey and I knew right away what they wanted. We started negotiating, and last night we paid them off. Fortunately, your money covered the whole ransom. Jolly good of you to do that."

You almost belt Ford in the mouth, but once again you realize there's nothing you can do. You're more dependent on Ford and Hickey than ever.

Just when you're thinking things couldn't get any worse, the animals finally collapse in a tiny oasis, still several days short of Cherchen. Seeing the state of your camels, no one at the oasis is willing to sell or hire out their animals to Ford and Hickey.

"I warned you," you can't resist taunting Ford. "Now what are we going to do?"

"I'll figure it out in the morning," he mutters.

Turn to page 5.

You buy a full box of manuscripts from Akhzur. Then you decide to move on from Turfan and keep looking for clues to Pinckney's whereabouts.

For two months you travel, through deserts from the Takla Makan to the Gobi, over hills from the Altyn Tagh to the Tangut. Although you compile a long list of sites for Montgomery to investigate, you fail to uncover a single clue to Pinckney or the Cave of a Thousand Buddhas. Your money—most of which you spent on the manuscripts—runs out, and you must return to London.

The baron finds the manuscripts fascinating. He says he's never seen anything like them, and that you may have discovered a lost language. He insists on buying all of them. You make a good profit.

However, several years later you're embarrassed when Montgomery, working at some of the sites you told him about, unmasks Akhzur as a forger and the manuscripts as fakes.

The End

You and Chan look at each other. "We'd have to sell off some of the gear we've bought," you say. "And we'd have to walk across the mountains, because our ponies would be carrying the balloon and supplies."

Chan rubs his chin for a few moments, then smiles. "Well . . . why not?"

You and Chan step to the side and figure out how much money you can raise between you, then come back to Haley with an offer. Haley accepts immediately.

"You won't be sorry," he says. "It's really quite a nifty contraption. Now, come back tomorrow morning and I'll show you how to assemble, inflate, and fly the thing."

You and Chan spend the next two days learning how to use your balloon. Then you pack it up with the rest of your supplies, find Norzen, your guide, and his assistants, and set off for the Karakoram.

Your small caravan climbs the path out of Srinagar through a forest of fir. You look back at the wide valley below. It will be months before you see civilization again.

For a week you travel over rock, glacier, and snow on faint roads, or on narrow trails clinging to the sides of thousand-foot gorges. At night you stay in little stone guest houses. After a long climb, you reach the pass of Tragbal. Stretching in front of you is the scribble of ridges and mountains you must cross to reach Sinkiang.

Turn to page 35.

"I'll take the Russian route," you say. "I want to get there quickly."

"All right," Montgomery replies. "But I hope you don't have trouble getting through. And be careful on the train. Unless you tip the porters rather generously, your baggage has a tendency to get 'lost.'"

"I'll remember that," you say.

"One more thing," Montgomery adds, going into his study to write a letter. "If you need help in Urumchi, you can call on my friend Macarthey. He's the British consul. Just give him this letter of introduction."

You tuck away the letter and thank Professor Montgomery. "Good luck," he calls as you walk down the steps.

The next day you leave for St. Petersburg. The Russian government doesn't give you any trouble over your passport, and soon you're on board a train for the long trip south. You make sure to give the porters a large tip so that your luggage will be transferred when you change trains.

So far your journey has been very smooth, except for one disturbing thing. Ever since London, a Chinese man has been following you—at least, he appears everywhere you go. You change trains in Moscow, and as your train pulls out, you again see the Chinese man. But he's left on the platform, arguing with the porters—about his luggage, you imagine.

Turn to page 28.

The next morning, following Islam Bai's advice, you take the long way around to Tun Huang. Several weeks later you arrive there. It's a relief, after miles of sand, to arrive in the green valley. You head straight for the caves Hedin described.

You wind your way along a river. Coming around a bend, you see hundreds of little grottoes carved into the cliffs on one side of the canyon.

You clamber up the cliffs. What you find astounds you. Cave after cave is filled with paintings, manuscripts, statues, sculptures, and rock-carved Buddhas, extremely well preserved. The treasures take your breath away.

At the top of the cliff you find a small temple, which is obviously inhabited by a monk. But no one is there, and no one comes during the week that you stay and sift through the contents of the caves. You decide you must get back to England to report your find to the baron.

On the long trip back across the Takla Makan and through India, you have time to think about the amazing objects in the caves. It seems a shame for them to become the property of only one man. Even though it means forfeiting the baron's reward, you decide to go to Montgomery instead of to the baron with your news.

When you find Montgomery in Persia, he's thrilled by your description of the caves. You both set off immediately for Tun Huang. A year later, after negotiating with the monk who lives in the temple, you return to Europe and receive widespread acclaim for your discovery.

The End

"I'll help you," you tell Pinckney.

"Here's the situation," Pinckney says. "Macarthey doesn't trust me. He doesn't really expect me to try to escape, either. He's watching this valley but none of the others. If I can get to the far side of the mountain, I can go down the other valley. All you have to do is have a horse and provisions for me there in five nights' time. I'll have a few more talks with Macarthey, then convince him I need a week of seclusion here before I can come down to Urumchi. I'll slip out at night, climb over the mountain, and meet you in the other valley."

"Okay," you say. "I think I can do that."

You say good-bye to Pinckney and prepare to ride down to Urumchi. On the way, you stop to tell Macarthey you must hurry back to London now that you've located Pinckney. You wish you didn't have to lie, but you can't see any way out of it.

In Urumchi you get a horse and provisions for Pinckney, turn around, and travel back up the valley on the other side of the mountain.

Pinckney arrives at the appointed place in the middle of the night. "Thank goodness you're here," he says. "After you left, I began to wonder if you would really help me."

He quickly gets onto the horse, then hands you a letter for the baron. "It explains—as much as possible—what's happened. It will also prove to the baron that you found me."

You wish Pinckney luck, and he rides off to his retreat beyond the Great Wall.

The End

You have a dream. One of the skeletons comes to life and begins to tell you his story. You see everything he says as if you were there.

His name was Fan, and he was a farmer in ancient times. He married a woman named Meng, and they lived happily in a valley in the mountains. But one day, soldiers came and took him away to help build the Great Wall. For years Fan labored hard with thousands of other men, piling stone upon stone as the wall was built mile by mile.

One year, as a harsh winter came on, Meng made a coat and sent it to Fan, along with a letter saying how much she missed him. The letter accidentally fell into the hands of the general in charge of building the wall. When he read the letter, he fell in love with Meng because of her beautifully written letter. He sent an aide to get her. In the meantime he decided he'd better do away with Fan. He sealed him in the wall, along with some workers who'd tried to desert.

Meng was taken to the general's tent where the general told her that a tragic accident had befallen Fan. "But don't worry," he said. "I will marry you and take care of you."

Meng was grief-stricken. She had no choice but to pretend to go along with the general. But on the way back to his palace for the wedding, she threw herself into the Yellow River and drowned.

Miraculously, the coat Meng had made for Fan survived. It is now in a monastery near the weeping stone, Fan says. If only someone would bring it to him, his soul could join Meng's in the next life.

Turn to page 39.

By now you're glad to have an excuse to get out of Peking. You book passage on the next ship out of Tientsin to England.

When you arrive, you go straight to the baron's estate and show him the form you received from the Chinese official. "I'm sorry to have to tell you this," you say, "but Pinckney is dead."

The baron studies the document carefully. "Did you see his body for yourself?"

"Well, no," you reply. "Once they informed me of Pinckney's death, the Chinese wouldn't give me permission to go any farther."

"Did you talk to anyone who knew Pinckney?" the baron asks.

"No," you say. "But the proof is there, in the document."

The baron leans back. "I'm sorry," he says. "I need more proof. I can't give you the reward."

The End

You go back to the Russian consulate to see if you can learn anything more about Mirmsk and Pogolosky. The front of the consulate is guarded, so you go around back and climb a tree next to the building.

As you go higher, reaching the second floor, you hear voices coming out of an open window. Silently you inch along a limb to get a view in the window. You see Mirmsk and Pogolosky inside, talking to a man behind a desk.

"We must find Pinckney!" the man proclaims. "We must find out how much he's told the British—"

Your eavesdropping is interrupted by a voice from below. "Hey! You in the tree! Get down here!" You look down. A guard has his rifle trained on you. You're caught!

Turn to page 114.

You ride your horse into the Bogda Ola. The next evening you reach the Heavenly Pool, a stunning clear blue mountain lake set in a fir-clad valley below the snowy summit of Bogda Feng.

You find Macarthey in a little inn on the near shore of the lake and present him with Montgomery's letter. He invites you to have dinner. The two of you discuss the adventures you've each had with your mutual friend Montgomery. Then Macarthey asks you the reason for your travel to Sinkiang. You explain about the baron's reward.

Macarthey's eyebrows arch when you mention Dr. Pinckney. He asks you to describe him, then says, "I wanted to make sure we're talking about the same person, because Dr. Pinckney is in the monastery on the other side of the lake."

"What—what's he doing here?" you stammer.

"As near as I can figure it, he's hiding out," Macarthey answers. "Besides being employed by the baron, Pinckney was an agent for the Russians— and a double agent for us."

You tell Macarthey about Mirmsk and Pogolosky. "That fits in," Macarthey says "Pinckney says the Russians have found him out. But he's also acting rather strangely—keeps going on about Taoism. Says he wants to become a monk. I wouldn't have known he was here, except that I heard a rumor and came up to find out what he was doing. I want to keep an eye on him until I do."

"Could I see him?" you ask.

"If he's agreeable," Macarthey replies." Maybe you can get some information out of him."

Turn to page 59.

You find a hidden spot outside of Tun Huang where you can tether the donkey. Then you go back into town. There, you hear that a caravan bound for Persia is coming through the next day. You decide to try to join it. Meanwhile, it grows dark, and you're exhausted. You return to where you left the donkey and fall asleep immediately.

When you wake up in the morning, the manuscripts are gone! At first you think Wang must have caught up with you somehow and taken them back at night. But by talking to people in the bazaar, you find out that the two foreigners—Ford and Hickey, no doubt—were asking where you were staying. They must have stolen the manuscripts!

You search angrily all over the town, but they've disappeared. Meanwhile, the caravan bound for Persia arrives. Realizing that Wang may be after you, and that with no money you'll never catch up with Ford and Hickey, you decide you'd better take this chance to get out of Sinkiang.

You're hired as a camel-tender on the caravan, and, many months later, track down Montgomery in Persia. He's glad to see that you're alive, but he has bad news. Word is already out that Ford and Hickey found the Cave of a Thousand Buddhas, collected the baron's reward, and are going to help him plunder it. You feel terrible about letting the manuscripts slip through your hands. You feel even worse about what you've done to Wang.

The End

The next day you tell Boroshin that you're sorry you must leave, but you want to get on with your search. A short while later you're knocking at the monastery door.

An old monk answers. He looks suspicious when you say you want to talk to the foreigner who recently arrived. "There is no foreigner here," he says, starting to close the door.

"Boroshin told me there was," you insist.

Hearing Boroshin's name, the monk opens the door. He disappears for a moment, then returns with the abbot. The abbot asks you question after question about how you got there.

"Well," he finally says, "I know of no Dr. Pinckney, but an Englishman named Smith did arrive the other day. I will allow you to see him."

As soon as you see Smith, you know he's Pinckney. You tell your story again.

"Well, you've found me," he admits. "However, it's essential that no one else knows I'm here. But you seem trustworthy. I don't see why you shouldn't collect the reward—if you agree to give part of it to the monastery, and agree not to reveal my whereabouts."

You agree happily to Pinckney's conditions. In return, he gives you a letter which will prove to the baron that you've found him.

The next day you head back to Boroshin's hut to see if he'll help finance your trip back to London in exchange for part of the reward. He gladly agrees—if you'll stay for a week and keep him company.

The End

According to legend, the hills were rat burrows. In ancient times, the rats saved the city by chewing up the leather harnesses and armor of an invading army of Huns. The Rat King is shown as a human figure with the crowned head of a rat, flanked by two attendants.

You trek back to Srinagar, where you wire Montgomery about your find. He wires back that he'll be with you as soon as he can. And so begins your career as an archaeologist.

The End

You know you could slip away from Ford and Hickey, but you also know you'd be in bad shape without your papers and money. You decide you'll have to go along with them and bide your time. They don't intend to harm you, they just want a partner who knows what's going on.

The three of you leave the next day to cross the Karakoram. It's a hard trip over snowy passes. Ford and Hickey drive the animals mercilessly. But in two weeks you're in Khotan, at the western edge of the Takla Makan.

All you find out about Pinckney in Khotan is that some of the other adventurers have been there before you. So you hire some camels and three Turki helpers to take you across the southern arm of the old Silk Route. You're disappointed to find that it's not much of a road, but instead a vague path marked only by dried bones.

Ford and Hickey continue to drive the animals—and everyone else—too hard. "You've got to take it easy going across the desert or our animals are never going to make it," you say.

Ford glares at you. "Who's in charge here, you or me?"

The weary caravan pushes on across the Takla Makan, stopping briefly at green oases every few days. The animals become weaker, and Ford lets up on them only because they, and you, are near collapse.

Go on to the next page.

You start to think you may somehow make it, though, when Cherchen is only eight days away. But then, one hot afternoon, you hear the sound of riders. A cloud of dust is moving across a ridge, headed straight at you.

"Bandits!" Hickey cries. He and Ford whip out their rifles and take aim. The Turkis and camels scatter in confusion. Montgomery's advice not to start any fights comes back to you, but you wonder if it applies now. You have only a few seconds to decide whether to try to stop Ford and Hickey from firing.

If you try to stop them, turn to page 74.

If you decide not to, turn to page 72.

After buying a horse to ride and a donkey to carry your gear, you set out, following a well-marked but less-traveled route through the Tien Shan Mountains.

The path starts from a lake, then climbs through dusty gulches into a cool forest. Eventually you come into high mountain meadows and grazing land, with snowcapped peaks towering above.

Suddenly, thundering out of the trees, comes a band of Mongol horsemen. You giddyup your horse into a gallop, leaving behind the donkey with your possessions. Most of the Mongols stop, surrounding your donkey. But one keeps coming after you. You look behind and see him smiling as he extends a long pole with a loop at the end. Suddenly, the loop is around your shoulders and you're pulled off your horse. Still smiling, the horseman leads you back to his comrades. One of them retrieves your horse while the rest take you to their mountain camp.

The camp consists of a group of yurts—large tent-like structures made of felts draped over collapsible wooden frames—in a meadow. Jasik, the Mongol who captured you, keeps you tied up in a corner of his yurt. You eat with his family, though, and you share their diet of mutton, cheese, tea with sour milk, rancid butter, and sugar.

As the days go by, you begin to wonder why the Mongols are holding you. Perhaps they plan to sell you into the slave trade. You manage to pick up enough of the language to ask Jasik what he plans to do with you. He smiles and says, "We'll see."

Turn to page 65.

During the next few days you help pack up camp. Soon the whole clan and its flocks are on their way out of the Tien Shan.

You drop down through the badlands with them, and a couple of weeks later come onto the steppes. You've never seen anything like them— great rolling green plains, featureless, endless. Your caravan seems tiny in the immense landscape.

By now you feel you can trust your Mongol captors enough to confide to them the reason for your journey. You ask if they've heard of Dr. Pinckney or know where the Cave of a Thousand Buddhas is.

"I have never heard of such a thing," Jasik responds. "But I will ask my kinsmen."

A little later Jasik returns and says, "We have heard many stories of haunted cities in the Ordos Desert, but never of a cave, nor anyone named Pinckney. However, there is someone else we can ask when we are near Urga. His name is Liang, and he is a Taoist hermit."

You cross the Yellow River, thick with the silt of the area which gives the river its name. It's this fine soil, you recall from your reading, which eons ago was blown off the steppes of Mongolia, leaving them barren, and into northern China, making it fertile.

You cross the bleak, brown Ordos, and, after fording the Yellow River once again, Jasik and some of his men take you a little way south to find the hermit Liang.

Turn to page 115.

You wait until Mirmsk and his friend have left for Urumchi, then you follow them on horseback at a safe distance. The road climbs a pass between the Tien Shan and Bogda Ola Mountains before dropping into Urumchi. From a high point above Urumchi, you watch the two Russians enter the gates and make their way to a building near the center of town.

You ride into town yourself and find the building. It's the Russian consulate, which doesn't help you very much. You decide to go to the British consulate and see if Montgomery's friend Macarthey can tell you anything.

But Macarthey isn't there. His secretary says he's vacationing in the Bogda Ola Mountains, at a place called the Heavenly Pool, a two-day ride from Urumchi.

You get directions, but you must decide whether you'd rather find Macarthey or stick with Mirmsk and Pogolosky. If you go up to the Heavenly Pool, you'll probably lose track of the Russians.

If you decide to go up to the Heavenly Pool, turn to page 86.

If you decide to stay in Urumchi and spy on the Russian consulate, turn to page 84.

One evening you pack some food and clothes on your horse and tell Jasik you're going out to check on the flocks. You ride out to the pasture. Then you just keep going, down through the meadows and forests, past the salt lake, and finally, two days later, into Urumchi.

You knock hungry and exhausted at Macarthey's door. A housekeeper answers, and you tell her that a friend of Macarthey's sent you there.

"I'm sorry," the housekeeper says. "Mr. Macarthey has taken off on some secret-agent chase." Then, seeing your state, she invites you in.

"Thank you," you say as you enter. "Do you know when he'll be back?"

"No one knows." She shrugs. "He left very quickly."

Macarthey's staff take care of you for a week, but you know you can't impose on the consul's hospitality much longer.

You see no choice but to give up your search for Pinckney. You manage to borrow money for your fare home. Once you do get to London, it'll take a while to raise the funds to try again. By then someone else may have claimed the reward.

The End

"I'm sorry," you say to Pinckney, "but I wouldn't feel right in helping you to get away."

"Oh, well," Pinckney says. "I suppose I can manage it myself. It'll just be that much trickier."

You say good-bye and go back to Macarthey's room at the inn. You sit down with him and say, "I think it's my duty to inform you of what I learned from Pinckney." You tell him Pinckney's story, and that he's planning to slip away.

Macarthey looks perplexed. "I suppose there's nothing I can do now but arrest him. I think he's a decent man, just a bit confused. I'm sorry to have to do it, but the authorities in London will have to sort the thing out. I'm sure they'll go easy on him."

But the authorities in London see things differently from Macarthey. Six months after your conversation with him, you're called in as a witness at Pinckney's trial for espionage. You try to explain that Pinckney didn't betray his country, he just got caught up in a complicated situation.

The judge listens, then says he'll be lenient; instead of execution he'll sentence Pinckney only to life imprisonment.

For the rest of your life, you're haunted by the thought that you've sent a good man to prison. Not only that, the baron refuses to pay a reward for a convicted spy.

The End

"Now you know why I am here," the *arhat* says. "Tell me why you are here."

You try to explain your interest in ruins, and your search for Pinckney.

After a few moments with his eyes closed, the *arhat* responds with a recommendation. "You must travel still farther. Go to the north and east, all the way to the Great Wall. Follow the old Tatung road to the weeping stone. Your destiny lies there."

"Thank you," you say. "Now I'll leave you in peace." He nods good-bye, and you back out of the room and through the halls of the labyrinth.

You find the pile of sand where you first arrived and start to scramble back up. You feel almost as if something is helping lift you out, and soon you're back on ground level.

That night in your camp, your experience starts to seem like a hallucination. Consulting your map, you see that Tatung is far away, in the northern part of China. You start to think that maybe you'll just ignore what the *arhat* said.

On the other hand, maybe you can't afford to.

If you decide to follow the arhat's *advice, turn to page 25.*

If you decide to keep looking around in the Lop Desert, turn to page 56.

"All right," Jasik says with a shrug. He tells you where to find the old road. Then he loads you up with provisions. You give him some medicines, and say farewell.

You set off into the hills. Soon you come across a faint old road overgrown with bushes. The country becomes more mountainous as you draw closer to the Great Wall. One night you stop at a farm and ask an old woman about the stone that weeps.

"Oh, yes, the weeping stone," the woman says. "No one goes there. It's haunted—that's why the road has been abandoned. This road will lead you right to it."

After two more days' travel, the Great Wall looms on the ridgetop. The road runs right into the wall, ending at what used to be a gate. Nearby, though the weather is dry, you find water seeping in a steady stream from a crack in the stone.

You walk up and down along the wall, looking for a way to get through. It's solid. You've seen no one for miles. You wonder what Liang was talking about.

Frustrated, you push at the wet stone. It moves. You push harder, and it swings open. You crawl inside. The stone swivels shut behind you.

You light a candle, and almost wish you hadn't. The first thing you see is a row of skeletons leaning against the wall of the chamber, seeming to grin at you. Picks, tools, and a few other objects are littered inside, but that's all you find.

Go on to the next page.

You start to feel nervous in the enclosed space. You push at the stones up and down the length of the chamber, looking for a way out. Nothing budges. The air is stifling. Suddenly you feel faint. You collapse on the ground.

Turn to page 82.

You don't have time for pursuing crazy dreams, you think as you hurry down the old road that continues on this side of the Great Wall.

As soon as you come to a modern road, you turn off and begin asking everyone you can find about Pinckney. But people seem unwilling to help you. They tell you nothing, and watch you suspiciously as you walk away.

After a few days your provisions run out. You become very hungry and must start begging for food. You have nowhere to go for help. Finally you decide your only hope for survival is to head for the desert and try to join a westbound caravan. If you're lucky, you'll make it to Persia and find Montgomery before you starve.

The End

Your eyes shut against the driving sand, you stand up and feel around for the gas to start letting the balloon down. The balloon, battered back and forth by the wind, is impossible to control. But you hold on as best you can, trying not to descend too quickly.

You have no idea how close the ground is, so you're completely surprised when a blast of wind dashes you, Chan, and the balloon to smithereens on a rocky outcropping.

The End

You float over the Takla Makan. Below you are the endless, rippling dunes. A caravan is inching across the desert like a caterpillar. In the distance you can see snowy mountains; above, a hot, clear blue sky.

A yellow haze is often kicked up by the wind, but when you can't see, you can navigate by compass. Crossing the Takla Makan takes days rather than weeks. "Think of all the things we're missing out on," Chan says. "Insects, snakes, bandits, thirst, hot sand, bureaucrats, soldiers."

The Tarim River and some low hills mark the end of the Takla Makan, and you enter the space over the Lop Desert. The salt bogs of Lop Nor pass below.

You're beginning to think you'll make it all the way to Ansi without mishap, when suddenly one afternoon the sky grows dark. A black cloud is coming toward you. "Is that a thunderstorm?" Chan wonders.

"No," you suddenly realize, "it's a *buran*!"

A few moments later, without warning, you're caught in a whirling mass of sand and pebbles. Everything becomes dark as the storm engulfs you. The wind howls like a demon, hurling debris in all directions. Strange clanging noises sound in the swirling mass of sand.

Go on to the next page.

You and Chan hide under blankets to escape the barrage. But you know you can't just stay where you are. The *buran* could last for hours, and the balloon will be destroyed in minutes. You must get out of the wind, either by trying to land or by trying to fly above the storm.

If you try to take the balloon down, turn to page 103.

If you try to take it up, turn to page 41.

When you return, you're relieved to hear that there is an answer. "However," the bureaucrat says, "I am sorry to tell you that permission to pass to Turfan has been denied. I have been informed that the Dr. Pinckney you seek is dead. Therefore, your trip is unnecessary."

You leave the office dejected. You wonder if Pinckney really is dead. If so, you could return to England and try to collect the baron's reward. But you could also try to slip over the northern border of China and trek through Mongolia to Turfan.

If you decide to return to England,
turn to page 83.

If you decide to slip across the Chinese border,
turn to page 109.

"Ah," Wang says, "the Silk Route. Like the pilgrim."

You know from your reading that he's talking about Hsüan-tsang, the Buddhist pilgrim, who traveled from China to India in the seventh century to find enlightenment. You discuss the travels of the pilgrim, who is also known as Tripitaka, because of the three baskets of manuscripts he brought back from India. Wang is delighted to find a fellow admirer of Hsüan-tsang who has journeyed the same route.

"You must come see the cave," Wang says, grabbing your sleeve with excitement. "There are copies of manuscripts translated by Tripitaka, and paintings of him as well."

"I would like nothing more," you say.

Turn to page 112.

You study your maps and decide to cross the border at Nankow Pass. From there you can make your way across Mongolia to Turfan.

You leave Peking the next day, relieved to be moving at last. You can't take trains because your passport is likely to be checked, so you go by foot. North of Peking you travel by cart to Nankow Pass.

Once you get to the pass, you realize that slipping across the border will not be as easy as you thought. You must cross the Great Wall. Obviously, you can't go through the gates, which are guarded. You have to figure out a way to get over the enormous stone barrier.

You decide you can climb it. The stones jut out enough to give you footholds and hand-holds. You'll be able to bring with you only what you can get in a rucksack, but you figure you can buy new supplies on the other side.

You wait until nightfall. Then you creep up to an unpatrolled part of the wall and begin to climb. At first it's pretty easy going. But as you get near the top, the handholds become smaller and smaller, and you can't see very well in the dark. Eventually, you mistake a dark spot for a handhold and lose your grip. You fall and break your neck.

The End

110

You book yourself on a ship to Peking right away. As the voyage goes on, and you come nearer to port in Tientsin, you notice fewer and fewer passengers on the ship. In Peking, people seem downright hostile. Finally a German man at your hotel explains that it's because of the Boxer Rebellion.

"What's that?" you ask.

"It's an uprising against foreign powers who have been forcing trade conditions on China," the man answers. "It's a dangerous time to be a Westerner here. I'd lay low until this thing passes over."

But you're impatient to get going. The next day you go down to the passport office and apply for an official pass to Turfan. The bureaucrat in charge wants to know every little detail about your trip. When you've finished telling him, he says he'll process your application as soon as possible.

You wait for a full week, then return to the passport office. The official is polite but cool. He says things are moving as quickly as can be expected. A week later you get the same bland answer.

"Perhaps," you hint, "there is a 'fee' I can pay?"

The official says that might help. You hand over a bribe, and he tells you to come back in a week.

Turn to page 107.

"Good," Montgomery replies. "I think the India route is the most promising."

You stay for dinner, then Montgomery shows you to the door and shakes your hand. "Good luck," he says. "I have to admit, I almost wish I were coming along."

Several months later you're making your way through the clamoring streets of Bombay to the train station. The ocean crossing went smoothly, except that several times you caught a glimpse of the face of a Chinese man. But every time you looked at him, he quickly disappeared. Now, in Bombay, you see him again. You can't help but wonder if he's following you.

A few more days on a train bring you to the city of Srinagar, in Kashmir, at the foot of the Karakoram Mountains. There you buy gear and supplies for your expedition. Montgomery's money helps you to buy a pony.

You're almost ready to leave. You've heard there's a caravan leaving in two weeks from Kashgar, on the other side of the Karakoram, to cross the Takla Makan. All you need to do the next day is buy a few more supplies and find a guide for the mountain crossing.

Turn to page 13.

112

All the next day you and Wang travel by donkey to the Cave of a Thousand Buddhas, arriving at dusk. The cave is actually a series of grottoes carved into a cliff which forms one side of a broad green canyon. Wang has built a little temple at the top of the cliff.

Wang takes you on a quick tour. You're amazed at what you see. There are hundreds of caves, filled with manuscripts, paintings, sculptures, and with friezes and Buddhas carved into the rock. "I am restoring all the caves," Wang says proudly, "and also protecting them from robbers and intruders."

After a simple dinner, Wang shows you to a guest room at the temple. "Tomorrow," he says, "you shall see more. But for now, sleep well."

You lie on your mat, but you can't sleep. You keep thinking about the treasures nearby. Wang is clearly proud of them, but he's also very protective. You wonder if you'll ever have another chance to convince Wang to let you take some of the treasures to England. You'd hate to betray Wang, but what if he sends you away tomorrow with nothing?

You could go out tonight, grab as many things as you can, and get away.

If you get up and sneak out to the caves, turn to page 60.

If you stay where you are, turn to page 71.

The guard marches you into the room you were just spying on, and explains to the three Russians what you were doing. "You again!" Mirmsk says. "I had a feeling you were a spy. Do you realize this building is the property of the Tsar's government?"

Mirmsk explains to the man behind the desk that you're also looking for Pinckney. "No doubt you are working for the English," the man says to you. "Unfortuantely we cannot deal with you here. We will have to send you back to Moscow for your trial for espionage."

Even if you're somehow found innocent, it'll be a long time before you can resume the search for Pinckney.

The End

Liang lives in a cave in the hills northwest of Tatung, near the Great Wall. He greets Jasik like an old friend.

You tell Liang what you're looking for. The hermit rubs his chin and decides, "I must throw the sticks."

You watch with fascination as he tosses a set of sticks on the ground, examines the way they fall, and mutters to himself. He repeats the process several times.

"I cannot tell you much," he says. "What I can tell you is that your destiny lies beyond the Great Wall, on a road no longer used. You should look for the place at the wall where the stone weeps."

"What does that mean?" you ask.

"I have told you what I know," Liang replies. "The rest is up to you."

You thank him and leave with Jasik. Jasik looks puzzled and says he's not sure what Liang was talking about, either. "There is an old road near here," he says. "It may lead to the wall, but then I do not know if you can get over it. Let some of my cousins take you. One way or another, they will get you across the wall."

You appreciate the offer, but you're not sure you want to accept. It sounds as if it could involve violence. Besides, Liang's words seem to suggest that you should go alone.

If you say, "I'll try to get over the wall alone,"
turn to page 100.

If you say you want Jasik's cousins to help you,
turn to page 11.

Still, you want some of the artifacts in the caves to come to light. "Maybe we can help each other out," you propose to Wang. "I have a friend named Montgomery who has many resources. I think he would be willing to make a large donation to your restoration work if you let us return and study the caves. We would promise not to reveal their location."

Wang's eyes light up at the mention of a donation. "That might be possible." He thinks for a moment. "Can you vouch for your friend Montgomery?"

"Completely," you say. "There's just one more thing. You have so many manuscripts here—could I take a few to show Montgomery?"

"Of course," Wang says.

Wang lends you one of the donkeys to get to Tun Huang the next day. You thank him, and say you'll be back within a year. In Tun Huang you join a caravan that is going all the way to Persia. There you track down Montgomery, who is thrilled by the manuscripts. He drops what he's doing and sets off with you for the Cave of a Thousand Buddhas.

The End

ABOUT THE AUTHOR

JAY LEIBOLD was born in Denver, Colorado. In the Choose Your Own Adventure series, he has also written *Sabotage, Grand Canyon Odyssey, Spy for George Washington, The Antimatter Formula,* and *Secret of the Ninja.*

ABOUT THE ILLUSTRATOR

YEE CHEA LIN is a graduate of Cooper Union in New York State. He is the illustrator of *Secret of the Sun God* in Bantam's Choose Your Own Adventure series.

Go On A Super Adventure in a Terrifying New World in the First Choose/Adventure® Superadventure!

January 14, 3000. You've been hibernating in a space capsule for a thousand years. Now you're awake and ready to return to the Earth of the future—but your computer has horrifying news to report. An evil tyrant named Styx Mori has proclaimed himself Supreme Emperor of Earth. He has agents everywhere—even on other planets. And no matter where you land, you face capture—and even death!

This Super Adventure has more—more of everything you like best about Bantam's Choose Your Own Adventure series! It's got more choices, more danger, more adventure—it's the biggest and best CYOA yet!

☐ *JOURNEY TO THE YEAR 3000: CYOA SUPER ADVENTURE #1 26157-6 $2.95 ($3.50 in Canada)*

Buy it at your local bookseller or use this page to order.
